POETRY FOR YOUNG PEOPLE

African American Poetry

Edited by Arnold Rampersad and Marcellus Blount • Illustrated by Karen Barbour

STERLING CHILDREN'S BOOKS
New York

STERLING CHILDREN'S BOOKS
New York

An Imprint of Sterling Publishing
387 Park Avenue South
New York, NY 10016

"Song of the Son" from *Cane* by Jean Toomer. Copyright © 1923 by Boni and Liveright, renewed 1951 by Jean Toomer. Used by permission of Liveright Publishing Corporation. ◈ "Tableau" by Countee Cullen. Copyrights held by Amistad Research Center, Tulane University, administered by Thompson and Thompson, Brooklyn, NY. ◈ "I, Too," "My People" from *The Collected Poems of Langston Hughes* by Langston Hughes, edited by Arnold Rampersad with David Roessel, Associate Editor, copyright © 1994 by the Estate of Langston Hughes. Used by permission of Alfred A. Knopf, a division of Random House, Inc. ◈ "Past the window pane" (haiku #37) and "The harbor at dawn" (haiku #64) copyright © 1998 by Ellen Wright. Reprinted from *Haiku: This Other World* by Richard Wright, published by Arcade Publishing, New York, New York. ◈ "Frederick Douglass." Copyright © 1966 by Robert Hayden, "The Moose Wallow," from *Collected Poems of Robert Hayden*, edited by Frederick Glaysher. Copyright © 1985 by Emma Hayden. ◈ "The Bean Eaters" and "Pete at the Zoo" by Gwendolyn Brooks, reprinted by consent of Brooks Permissions. ◈ "I Want to Write" by Margaret Walker from *This Is My Century: New and Collected Poems* by Margaret Walker, © 1989 by Margaret Walker Alexander, published by The University of Georgia Press, Athens, Georgia, 30602. All rights reserved. ◈ "The Nature of This Flower Is to Bloom" from *Revolutionary Petunias & Other Poems*, copyright © 1973 by Alice Walker, reprinted by permission of Houghton Mifflin Harcourt Publishing Company. ◈ "Winter Poem" from *My House* by Nikki Giovanni copyright © 1972 by Nikki Giovanni, renewed 2000 by Nikki Giovanni. Reprinted by permission of HarperCollins Publishers. ◈ "A Round," "Poem No. 1," from *How I Got Ovah* by Carolyn M. Rodgers, copyright © 1968, 1969, 1970, 1972, 1973, 1975 by Carolyn M. Rodgers. Used by permission of Doubleday, a division of Random House, Inc. ◈ "My Father's First Baseball Game," and "A Meditation for My Son" from *My Father's Geography* by Michael S. Weaver © 1992. Reprinted by permission of the University of Pittsburgh Press. ◈ Lucille Clifton, "the poet" from *Good Woman: Poems and a Memoir 1969–1980.* Copyright © 1987 by Lucille Clifton. Reprinted with the permission of BOA Editions, Ltd. ◈ "Imagination" © 1985 by James Baldwin is collected in *Jimmy's Blues*, published by St. Martin's. Reprinted by arrangement with the James Baldwin Estate. ◈ "Caged Bird," copyright © 1983 by Maya Angelou from *Shaker, Why Don't You Sing?* by Maya Angelou. Used by permission of Random House, Inc. ◈ "Alone" from *Songlines in Michaeltree: New and Collected Poems.* Copyright © 2000 by Michael S. Harper. Used with permission of the poet and the University of Illinois Press. ◈ "plum blossom plum jam" copyright © 2005 by June Jordan Literary Estate trust, reprinted by permission. www.junejordan.com ◈ "Offspring" from *Pink Ladies in the Afternoon* by Naomi Long Madgett. Copyright © 1972. Reprinted by permission of the author and Lotus Press. ◈ "Obsidian" by Melvin Dixon, published 1995 in *Love's Instruments* by Tia Chucha Press, San Fernando, CA. All Rights Reserved. ◈ "Apollo" by Elizabeth Alexander, published 1996 in *Body of Life* by Tia Chucha Press, San Fernando, CA. All Rights Reserved.

ISBN 978-1-4027-1689-8

Distributed in Canada by Sterling Publishing
c/o Canadian Manda Group, 165 Dufferin Street
Toronto, Ontario, Canada M6K 3H6

For information about custom editions, special sales, and premium and corporate purchases, please contact Sterling Special Sales at 800-805-5489 or specialsales@sterlingpublishing.com.

Manufactured in China

Lot #:
2 4 6 8 10 9 7 5 3 1
10/12
www.sterlingpublishing.com/kids

Contents

Introduction

Phillis Wheatley dared to believe that she could be a poet. Taken by force from Africa to America in 1761 as a child of seven or eight years, Wheatley was sold to a Boston gentleman to be a servant in his house. She faced a world that typically—though not in every case—had harsh opinions of black people, who were seen as useful only as common laborers. In many parts of America it was a crime to teach a black person to read or write. The family Phillis Wheatley worked for had different ideas. Educated by her owners, Wheatley began to write poetry while still a girl (see her poem "On Being Brought from Africa to America," p. 8) and grew up to be a devout Christian. In 1773 she published *Poems on Various Subjects, Religious and Moral*. This was only the second book of poems published by an American woman and the very first by an African American.

For a long time after Wheatley died in 1784, black American poetry hardly developed. Then a slave, George Moses Horton in North Carolina, who was allowed a degree of freedom by his slave owner, composed three books of verse. They included *The Hope of Liberty* (1829) and *The Poetical Works of George M. Horton: The Colored Bard of North Carolina* (1845). Horton became the first black poet to use poetry to attack slavery directly. "George Moses Horton, Myself" (p. 9) speaks to his personal ambition as a writer and about the obstacles in his way. Many white people thought of the black poet as someone reaching above his or her "natural" place in life. How, they asked, could slaves and their descendants think of themselves as poets and produce works of literature worthy of attention? It took extreme courage to be a black writer during that time.

Wheatley and Horton are alike in seeing their poetry as a chance to assert their interests apart from the subject of race and also to defend the humanity of African Americans as best they could. These two writers set the key challenges for future African American poets. On the one hand, the black poet must insist on the freedom to write on any and all subjects. On the other hand, the African American poet often feels an obligation to write about the injustices blacks faced and continue to face.

Frances Ellen Watkins Harper, born free in Maryland during the age of slavery, took a bolder approach. She became a crusader for social justice. Her antislavery zeal may be seen in her book *Poems on Miscellaneous Subjects* (1854). Thus began decades of opposition to slavery and, when slavery was abolished, opposition to segregation and to injustice everywhere. For example, her "Songs for the People" (p. 10) does not specify black Americans at any point. Harper is protesting against war and poverty in general, on behalf of the young as well as the old. Her alertness to injustices suffered by black people made her sensitive to injustices suffered by all of humanity.

Most Americans paid little attention to the work of black poets until near the end of the nineteenth century when Ohio-born Paul Laurence Dunbar began publishing his work. His polished language, as seen here in "We Wear the Mask" (p. 12) and "Dawn" (p. 13), delighted readers. Dunbar was also well known for his poetry in dialect—composed in imitation of the speech of uneducated, mainly country black folk. But when it became clear that most readers preferred his dialect poetry to his poetry in Standard English, he became unhappy. Dunbar believed that these dialect poems gave a misleading, usually comic view of black American life. Other black poets who wrote dialect verse but also composed in Standard English faced the same problem.

The start of the twentieth century saw a major change in African American culture. This change was caused mainly by the so-called Great Migration of blacks out of the South, where the vast majority had lived, to the cities of the North. (On this topic, see Claude McKay's "To One Coming North," p. 14.) In the North, jobs were easier to come by and better paid. In general, racial segregation was also less of an issue. As a result, black communities in the North took root. The arts, including poetry but also music such as jazz and the blues, flourished as never before.

This era is often called the Harlem Renaissance, because so many of the best African American writers, artists, and musicians lived for a while in Harlem, a vibrant neighborhood in New York City. New York was also the location of most of the top publishers and the magazines in which much of the new poetry first appeared. The major poets of this period represented in this anthology include Claude McKay, Langston Hughes ("I, Too," p. 21, and "My People," p. 48), Countee Cullen ("Tableau," p. 20), and James Weldon Johnson ("The Creation," pp. 22–25).

The younger writers of this era wanted to be free from all restrictions imposed on them. They also wanted to challenge black people who were ashamed of certain parts of African American culture and believed that poets should avoid anything that did not show the black community in a flattering light. Langston Hughes and others objected to such pressures. They wanted to show black life as it really was. As Hughes put it in a famous essay, "The Negro Artist and the Racial Mountain" (1926), the new writers intended "to express our individual dark-skinned selves without fear or shame. . . . We build our temples for tomorrow . . . and we stand on top of the mountain, free within ourselves."

The Harlem Renaissance ended early in the 1930s, when mass poverty swept the United States into the Great Depression. This decade produced few major volumes of black poetry, but the next decade was more fruitful. In 1942, Margaret Walker, an admirer of Langston Hughes, won an important award, the Yale Series of Younger Poets prize, for her little volume *For My People*. This book was expressly inspired by the African American community (as is her poem "I Want to Write," p. 32). But even more influential and admired were Robert Hayden (see his "Frederick Douglass," p. 28, and "The Moose Wallow," p. 29) and Gwendolyn Brooks ("Pete at the Zoo," p. 30, and "The Bean Eaters," p. 31).

After reading deeply in African American history, Hayden wrote some of the most brilliant poetry of the century, including his tribute to Frederick Douglass (born a slave and thought by many to be the leading black American of the nineteenth century). As we see in "The Moose Wallow" (p. 29), Hayden also wrote verse that avoids race and politics to deal instead with ideas and feelings common to most people everywhere. In 1950, Gwendolyn Brooks won the Pulitzer Prize for poetry for her book *Annie Allen* (1949). This was the highest literary honor ever awarded to an African American.

Brooks combined a deep love of black people, especially those who lived in her native Chicago, with an interest in modernism, an approach to writing that often involves the use of complex, challenging language. She could write with pure simplicity (as in "Pete at the Zoo," p. 30), but elsewhere her meaning is somewhat harder to grasp. In "The Bean Eaters" (p. 31), for example, what is her attitude to the couple in the poem? Does she admire them? Or is she merely observing them with pity in their old age and poverty?

In later years, starting in the 1960s, black American poetry and culture further changed. Younger poets set about expressing themselves with a freedom never before seen in African American poetry—not even during the Harlem Renaissance. Many of them wrote with a sense of pride and determination that would have astonished their ancestors. Their boldness was encouraged by the U.S. Supreme Court decision of 1954 that struck down school segregation and by the civil rights struggle led by Dr. Martin Luther King, Jr. Around 1965, a whole new group of poets emerged after the sudden rise of the idea of Black Power, which often emphasized the need for African Americans to separate themselves from the white community.

In the 1960s and 1970s, poetry became more popular than ever before. Many of the new writers wrote works that mainly expressed anger and even rage at racial prejudice. This powerful energy broke down certain older ways of writing poems. Black poetry moved increasingly toward free verse, with little or no interest in rhyme, traditional punctuation, and other forms that restricted the poet.

Eventually anger and rage gave way to quieter but no less effective approaches. These changes are well represented in the poems chosen here from writers such as Alice Walker, Lucille Clifton, Naomi Long Madgett, Carolyn M. Rodgers, June Jordan, and Nikki Giovanni, among writers who established themselves in the 1960s, and Michael S. Weaver (now known as Afaa Michael Weaver) and Elizabeth Alexander, who came later.

In "The Nature of This Flower Is to Bloom" (p. 33), for example, Alice Walker writes of "revolutionary petunias." Revolutions (the overthrowing of governments, usually by people who have been oppressed by them) often come about through violence. But in this poem, revolution is represented by the refusal of a certain common flower to wither and die in the face of the strong forces all around it. Is Walker asking us to see ordinary black people as tough but beautiful flowers that stand their ground against the world? When Melvin Dixon writes in "Obsidian" (p. 45) about an unusually hard form of black glass created by volcanoes, does he want to remind us of the African American people? When June Jordan tells us in "plum blossom plum jam" (p. 43) about a tree that seems dead but then almost miraculously blooms and bears delicious fruit, is she also telling us something about black people? Or does she mean for us to read in her poem a statement about human beings everywhere? Is "Poem No. 1" (p. 37) by Carolyn M. Rodgers about African Americans only or about the world in general? The same questions might be asked of Maya Angelou and her poem "Caged Bird" (p. 42).

Sometimes black poets go even further in detaching themselves from race as a subject. In

"Winter Poem" (p. 35), for example, Nikki Giovanni enters into a fantasy about being completely at one with nature in the snow and then in the spring rain that follows. Note how the absence of any punctuation in the poem enhances our sense of the poet's pure happiness. In "Offspring" (p. 44), Naomi Long Madgett sees her plans and dreams about her daughter give way to the girl's own ideas about what she wants to do with her life. In the end, the poet is proud of her child's independence and mature judgment—and parents everywhere have been taught a lesson, perhaps, about trusting their children. In "The Poet" (p. 40), Lucille Clifton reveals the extent to which she sees poetry as coming from troubling forces in her mind that cannot be denied. Isn't there a lesson here for everyone? Carolyn M. Rodgers's "A Round" (p. 36) has a similar theme to which many people can relate. Often one must struggle to understand life. There is usually no shortcut to getting to the heart of a serious matter.

If these and other African American poets frequently write without reference to race, just as often the past of slavery and segregation and the pain of life under injustice continue to be features of black poetry. When Afaa Michael Weaver writes in "My Father's First Baseball Game" (p. 38) about attending the event with his father, the sad past is upon us. His father can't forget the days when black people were not allowed to play in the Major Leagues and often were not even allowed to sit among white people in the stands. Similarly, in "Apollo" (p. 46), Elizabeth Alexander cannot write about watching the first men land on the moon in 1969 without setting that historic moment against the discomfort of her family seeing the event on television in a roadside restaurant where they know they are perhaps not wanted as customers because of their skin color.

Thus we see African American poets continuing to follow the trail first blazed by Phillis Wheatley as a girl in Boston more than two centuries ago. She wanted to write both about herself as a person of African descent who experienced hardships in America and about herself as a human being who loved poetry and the world around her. She wanted to write about the present and the past, sadness and joy, black and white, men and women, herself and others. Above all, she wanted to be a poet. For more than two hundred years, African American poets have accepted the same responsibilities she did, sought the same freedom to express themselves, and often worked against severe odds to do so. In the process, these writers have created a precious, powerful, and ever-evolving body of work.

Arnold Rampersad
Stanford University

On Being Brought from Africa to America

Phillis Wheatley (circa 1753–1784)

Wheatley was brought by force as a young girl from West Africa to America and was sold to a Boston family. She worked as a servant in the family's home but spent almost every free moment learning to read and write. She converted to Christianity and decided early to become a poet. In her writing, she celebrated the lives of prominent people such as George Washington, who met and encouraged her. She also wrote about the distinction between right and wrong and other aspects of philosophy. In this poem, she combines her love of Christianity with her concern for the fate of black people in America. She proposes to her readers that by converting to Christianity, black people and white people are equal in God's eyes.

'Twas mercy brought me from my *Pagan* land,
Taught my benighted soul to understand
That there's a God, that there's a *Saviour* too:
Once I redemption neither sought nor knew.
Some view our sable race with scornful eye,
"Their colour is a diabolic die."
Remember, *Christians*, *Negros*, black as *Cain*,
May be refin'd, and join th' angelic train.

pagan—*someone who is not Christian, Jewish, or Muslim*
benighted—*ignorant*
redemption—*state of being saved from hell*
sable—*black*

diabolic—*of the Devil*
die—*an artificial coloring (dye)*
Cain—*In the Bible, Cain murders his brother, Abel.*
train—*company*

George Moses Horton, Myself

George Moses Horton (1797–1884)

Born a slave in North Carolina, Horton became the first black American to use verse to argue directly against slavery. His slave holders gave him unusual freedom to develop as a writer. He often earned money by writing love poems for young men who wanted to woo their favorite lady friends. At the same time, he wrote poems opposing slavery. Eventually he published three books of poetry. In this poem, Horton never mentions slavery and racism, but they are surely the main factors that prevent him from expressing himself freely.

I feel myself in need
    Of the inspiring strains of ancient lore,
My heart to lift, my empty mind to feed,
    And all the world explore.

I know that I am old
    And never can recover what is past,
But for the future may some light unfold
    And soar from ages blast.

I feel resolved to try,
    My wish to prove, my calling to pursue,
Or mount up from the earth into the sky,
    To show what Heaven can do.

My genius from a boy,
    Has fluttered like a bird within my heart;
But could not thus confined her powers employ,
    Impatient to depart.

She like a restless bird,
    Would spread her wings, her power to be unfurl'd,
And let her songs be loudly heard,
    And dart from world to world.

lore—*history*
blast—*unhappy*

9

Songs for the People

Frances Ellen Watkins Harper (1825–1911)

Harper, who was born in Baltimore, Maryland, wrote many novels, books of poetry, essays, and stories. She became one of the most respected African American writers of the nineteenth century. As a young woman she worked as a school-teacher before devoting herself to the antislavery movement. Without mentioning race or racism in "Songs for the People," she expresses her wish to write poetry that comforts and inspires humanity.

Let me make the songs for the people,
    Songs for the old and young;
Songs to stir like a battle-cry
    Wherever they are sung.

Not for the clashing of sabres,
    For carnage nor for strife;
But songs to thrill the hearts of men
    With more abundant life.

Let me make the songs for the weary,
    Amid life's fever and fret,
Till hearts shall relax their tension,
    And careworn brows forget.

Let me sing for little children,
    Before their footsteps stray,
Sweet anthems of love and duty,
    To float o'er life's highway.

I would sing for the poor and aged,
    When shadows dim their sight;
Of the bright and restful mansions,
    Where there shall be no night.

Our world, so worn and weary,
    Needs music, pure and strong,
To hush the jangle and discords
    Of sorrow, pain, and wrong.

Music to soothe all its sorrow,
    Till war and crime shall cease;
And the hearts of men grown tender
    Girdle the world with peace.

sabres—*swords*
carnage—*bloodshed*
girdle—*embrace and hold tight*

We Wear the Mask

Paul Laurence Dunbar (1872–1906)

Dunbar was the only African American student in his high school in Dayton, Ohio, but he became president of his graduating class. Racial discrimination barred him from jobs that reflected his intelligence and learning. He became an elevator operator in Dayton. Nevertheless, with the encouragement of white and black friends he published books of poetry that earned him national recognition. He wrote both "dialect" verse and highly polished poems in Standard English. His poem here stresses the deception that life forces on most people. Even as fear, sadness, or pain afflicts us, we feel the need to present a smiling face to the world. His poem nowhere mentions racism, but we may assume that he is referring here to the false face that black people had to present to the white community in Dunbar's time, when racial segregation was the law of the land.

We wear the mask that grins and lies,
It hides our cheeks and shades our eyes,—
This debt we pay to human guile;
With torn and bleeding hearts we smile,
And mouth with myriad subtleties,

Why should the world be over-wise,
In counting all our tears and sighs?
Nay, let them only see us, while
    We wear the mask.

We smile, but, O great Christ, our cries
To Thee from tortured souls arise.
We sing, but oh the clay is vile
Beneath our feet, and long the mile;
But let the world dream otherwise,
    We wear the mask!

● ● ●

guile—*trickery*
myriad—*many*
subtleties—*tricks*

Dawn

In another exquisitely written poem, Dunbar imagines the moment in the early
morning when darkness finally gives way to sunlight.

An angel, robed in spotless white,
Bent down and kissed the sleeping Night.
Night woke to blush; the sprite was gone.
Men saw the blush and called it Dawn.

sprite—*a spirit or ghost; in this poem, an angel*

To One Coming North

Claude McKay (1889–1948)

*Early in the twentieth century, thousands of black people moved
from the southern states and from the Caribbean to work and
live in the major northern cities of America. McKay, who was
born in Jamaica in the West Indies, was one of them. In 1912 he
came to the United States and studied agriculture in Alabama
and Kansas before moving to New York. Like other migrants, he
was looking for better jobs and greater freedom. In New York City
he published two books of poetry that influenced many younger
African American writers as part of what came to be known as the
Harlem Renaissance. Although several of his poems attack racism
in America as a whole, in this poem McKay stresses the welcoming
embrace of the North.*

At first you'll joy to see the playful snow,
    Like white moths trembling on the tropic air,
Or waters of the hills that softly flow
    Gracefully falling down a shining stair.

And when the fields and streets are covered white
    And the wind-worried void is chilly, raw,
Or underneath a spell of heat and light
    The cheerless frozen spots begin to thaw,

Like me you'll long for home, where birds' glad song
    Means flowering lanes and leas and spaces dry,
And tender thoughts and feelings fine and strong,
    Beneath a vivid silver-flecked blue sky.

But oh! more than the changeless southern isles,
    When Spring has shed upon the earth her charm,
You'll love the Northland wreathed in golden smiles
    By the miraculous sun turned glad and warm.

✳✳✳

you'll joy—*you'll be joyful*
void—*emptiness*
leas—*fields*

The Black Finger

....

Angelina Weld Grimké (1880–1958)

Grimké spent her early years in and around Boston. Later she taught school in Washington, D.C., before moving to New York. There she was admired as the author of several published poems and one successful play, Rachel, *about a young woman's painful experience of racial discrimination. Her poem here is in free verse— unrhymed and with lines of varying length—as had become common in the modern era of poetry. Although it never mentions race as a topic, it perhaps links the silhouette or outline of a beautiful, dark cypress tree to the rising hopes and dreams of black people.*

I have just seen a beautiful thing
Slim and still,
Against a gold, gold sky,
A straight, black cypress,
Sensitive
Exquisite
A black finger
Pointing upwards.
Why, beautiful still finger are you black?
And why are you pointing upwards?

cypress—*an evergreen tree known for its dark foliage*

Exultation

Mae V. Cowdery (1909–1953)

Cowdery was born in Philadelphia, where she lived before moving to New York. While she did not publish a book of poems, her writing was admired by some of the best artists of the Harlem Renaissance. Like Angelina Weld Grimké's "The Black Finger," Cowdery's "Exultation" is written in free verse and does not overtly mention race. The speaker of the poem reminds us that both the day and the night are beautiful and that we should celebrate them equally despite their differences.

O day!
With sun glowing—
Gold
Pouring through
A scarlet rustling tree!

O night!
With stars burning—
Fire falling
Into a dark and whispering sea!

Song of the Son

Jean Toomer (1894–1967)

Born in Washington, D.C., Toomer attended college in New York City, among other places. In 1921, a four-month visit to Sparta, Georgia, had the biggest impact on his writing career. Out of that visit came Toomer's amazing book of poetry and fiction Cane *(1923), in which this poem appears. Set in the South, "Song of the Son" celebrates the finer aspects of the old-time black culture of African Americans as they suffered under the hardships of bondage and racial segregation.*

Pour O pour that parting soul in song,
O pour it in the sawdust glow of night,
Into the velvet pine-smoke air tonight,
And let the valley carry it along.
And let the valley carry it along.

O land and soil, red soil and sweet-gum tree,
So scant of grass, so profligate of pines,
Now just before an epoch's sun declines
Thy son, in time, I have returned to thee,
Thy son, I have in time returned to thee.

In time, for though the sun is setting on
A song-lit race of slaves, it has not set;
Though late, O soil, it is not too late yet
To catch thy plaintive soul, leaving, soon gone,
Leaving, to catch thy plaintive soul soon gone.

O Negro slaves, dark purple ripened plums,
Squeezed, and bursting in the pine-wood air,
Passing, before they stripped the old tree bare
One plum was saved for me, one seed becomes

An everlasting song, a singing tree,
Caroling softly souls of slavery,
What they were, and what they are to me,
Caroling softly souls of slavery.

sawdust—*from cutting down pine trees for lumber*
pine-smoke—*from burning the sawdust*
profligate—*plentiful*

epoch—*an important period of history*
caroling—*singing*

Tableau

For Donald Duff
Countee Cullen (1903–1946)

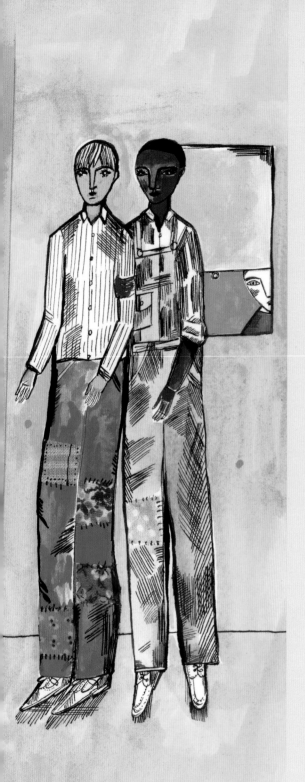

The adopted son of a prominent Harlem minister, Cullen was one of the leading young talents of the Harlem Renaissance in New York City. He loved poetry but felt the sting of racism keenly. In one poem he wrote about how odd it is for God "To make a poet black, and bid him sing!" But sing Cullen did as a poet. He favored traditional poetic forms, including rhyme and stanzas, as we see in "Tableau." Here he defends integration. Although black and white adults seem to disapprove of the close friendship between these two children, the boys reject this attitude without thinking much about it. They refuse to become timid or fearful as a result of the disapproval of other people.

Locked arm in arm they cross the way,
　　The black boy and the white,
The golden splendor of the day,
　　The sable pride of night.

From lowered blinds the dark folk stare,
　　And here the fair folk talk,
Indignant that these two should dare
　　In unison to walk.

Oblivious to look and word
　　They pass, and see no wonder
That lightning brilliant as a sword
　　Should blaze the path of thunder.

tableau—*a picture*
sable—*black*
unison—*unity*
oblivious—*unaware*

I, Too

....

Langston Hughes (1902–1967)

*Born in Joplin, Missouri, Hughes grew up in Lawrence, Kansas, and
Cleveland, Ohio, before spending a year in Mexico. He then went
to New York to attend Columbia University and become one of the
founders of the Harlem Renaissance. He blended into his poetry
African American cultural forms such as blues and jazz. In this free
verse poem, however, he echoes a famous poem, "I Hear America
Singing," by Walt Whitman, a leading white American poet Hughes
deeply admired. Here Hughes insists on the right of black Americans
to claim the United States as their country even if many white
people seem to want to deny them that right. Happy to be black,
the speaker of the poem is confident that one day he and other
black Americans will find peace and justice in America. In another
poem, "My People," which closes this book, Hughes declares his
unconditional love of all black people.*

    I, too, sing America.

    I am the darker brother.
    They send me to eat in the kitchen
    When company comes,
    But I laugh,
    And eat well,
    And grow strong.

    Tomorrow,
    I'll be at the table
    When company comes.
    Nobody'll dare
    Say to me,
    "Eat in the kitchen,"
    Then.

    Besides,
    They'll see how beautiful I am
    And be ashamed—

    I, too, am America.

The Creation

James Weldon Johnson (1871–1938)

Born in Jacksonville, Florida, Johnson was one of the oldest of the influential writers of the Harlem Renaissance. By the time he wrote "The Creation," Johnson was well known as a U.S. diplomat, a songwriter, a poet, a novelist, an anthologist, an essayist, and a civil rights leader. In this poem, a black preacher tells the story of the making of the world. His main guide is the Book of Genesis in the Bible. Using the sacred text as his basis, the preacher creates for his congregation a God who is very much like a normal human being despite possessing supernatural powers.

And God stepped out on space,
And he looked around and said:
I'm lonely—
I'll make me a world.

And far as the eye of God could see
Darkness covered everything,
Blacker than a hundred midnights
Down in a cypress swamp.

Then God smiled,
And the light broke,
And the darkness rolled up on one side,
And the light stood shining on the other,
And God said: That's good!

Then God reached out and took the light in his hands,
And God rolled the light around in his hands
Until he made the sun;
And he set that sun a-blazing in the heavens.
And the light that was left from making the sun
God gathered it up in a shining ball

And flung it against the darkness,
Spangling the night with the moon and stars.
Then down between
The darkness and the light
He hurled the world;
And God said: That's good!

Then God himself stepped down—
And the sun was on his right hand,
And the moon was on his left;
The stars were clustered about his head,
And the earth was under his feet.
And God walked, and where he trod
His footsteps hollowed the valleys out
And bulged the mountains up.

Then he stopped and looked and saw
That the earth was hot and barren.
So God stepped over to the edge of the world
And he spat out the seven seas—
He batted his eyes, and the lightnings flashed—
He clapped his hands, and the thunders rolled—
And the waters above the earth came down,
The cooling waters came down.

Then the green grass sprouted,
And the little red flowers blossomed,
The pine tree pointed his finger to the sky,
And the oak spread out his arms,
The lakes cuddled down in the hollows of the ground,
And the rivers ran down to the sea;
And God smiled again,
And the rainbow appeared,
And curled itself around his shoulder.

Then God raised his arm and he waved his hand
Over the sea and over the land,
And he said: Bring forth! Bring forth!
And quicker than God could drop his hand,
Fishes and fowls
And beasts and birds
Swam the rivers and the seas,
Roamed the forests and the woods,
And split the air with their wings.
And God said: That's good!

Then God walked around,
And God looked around
On all that he had made.
He looked at his sun,
And he looked at his moon,
And he looked at his little stars;
He looked on his world
With all its living things,
And God said: I'm lonely still.

Then God sat down—
On the side of a hill where he could think;
By a deep, wide river he sat down;
With his head in his hands,
God thought and thought,
Till he thought: I'll make me a man!

Up from the bed of the river
God scooped the clay;
And by the bank of the river
He kneeled him down;
And there the great God Almighty
Who lit the sun and fixed it in the sky,
Who flung the stars to the most far corner of the night,
Who rounded the earth in the middle of his hand;
This Great God,
Like a mammy bending over her baby,
Kneeled down in the dust
Toiling over a lump of clay
Till he shaped it in his own image;

Then into it he blew the breath of life,
And man became a living soul.
Amen.   Amen.

cypress—*an evergreen tree known for its dark foliage*
barren—*bare*
mammy—*a term once used for a motherly black woman*

[Haiku]

Richard Wright (1908–1960)

Wright, born on a plantation near Natchez, Mississippi, grew up in the South, moved to Chicago in 1927, and then relocated to New York. Works such as his novel Native Son *(1940) and his autobiography,* Black Boy *(1945), made him internationally famous. These works deal with the violence and hatred caused by racism in both the white and black communities. Eventually he emigrated to France. Generally unknown in his lifetime as a poet, he nevertheless quietly wrote hundreds of "haiku," which were published after his death. A classic, tightly disciplined Japanese form, a proper haiku consists of three unrhymed lines. Each of the first and third lines must have five syllables; the second line must have seven syllables. The subject is almost always nature.*

37
Past the window pane
A solitary snowflake
Spins furiously.

64
The harbor at dawn:
The faint scent of oranges
On gusts of March wind.

Frederick Douglass
....
Robert Hayden (1913–1980)

Born in Detroit, Hayden experienced a youth there that was shaped by troubles at home but also by severe eye problems. Nevertheless he read widely and deeply. Eventually he delved into African American history, which would be reflected in his best poetry. "Frederick Douglass" is an example of this influence. The poem, an unrhymed version of the sonnet form (which traditionally calls for fourteen rhyming lines), reflects that reading. Born a slave, Frederick Douglass became one of the bravest and brightest opponents of slavery as well as a champion of women's rights. He was arguably the most honored African American of the nineteenth century. This tribute poem stresses our need to live according to Douglass's ideals of hope, bravery, freedom, and love.

When it is finally ours, this freedom, this liberty, this beautiful
and terrible thing, needful to man as air,
usable as earth; when it belongs at last to all,
when it is truly instinct, brain matter, diastole, systole,
reflex action; when it is finally won; when it is more
than the gaudy mumbo jumbo of politicians:
this man, this Douglass, this former slave, this Negro
beaten to his knees, exiled, visioning a world
where none is lonely, none hunted, alien,
this man, superb in love and logic, this man
shall be remembered. Oh, not with statues' rhetoric,
not with legends and poems and wreaths of bronze alone,
but with the lives grown out of his life, the lives
fleshing his dream of the beautiful, needful thing.

diastole—*when the heart muscles relax and draw in blood*   mumbo jumbo—*insincere speech*
systole—*when the heart muscles contract and expel blood*   fleshing—*giving substance to something*

The Moose Wallow

In addition to poems about African American history such as "Frederick Douglass," Hayden wrote many poems of a more personal nature. Here the speaker of his poem admits that he is conflicted about the huge, almost mysterious moose lurking in the dark as he walks on a path in the country. The thought of a moose's size and wildness terrifies him, but he also wants to see for himself a creature of such rare power.

Friends warned of moose that
often came to the wallow
near the path I took.

I feared, hoped to see
the tall ungainly creatures
in their battle crowns.

I felt their presence
in the dark (hidden watchers)
on either side.

wallow—a muddy or dusty place, often created by
animals for their pleasure
battle crowns—antlers

Pete at the Zoo

Gwendolyn Brooks (1917–2000)

Topeka, Kansas, was the birthplace of Brooks, but within a few weeks after her birth, she and her parents moved to Chicago, where she lived the rest of her life. The city would be a powerful source of inspiration in a career that started when she was a child. Eventually she would be seen as one of the finest African American poets of all time. Many of her poems are complex and challenging, but others, such as "Pete at the Zoo," are relatively straightforward. A boy named Pete asks himself a question that points to his sympathy for a beast. Is the elephant in the zoo, so powerful with his massive body, really much different from a little boy or girl when the elephant is alone in the zoo at night?

I wonder if the elephant
Is lonely in his stall
When all the boys and girls are gone
And there's no shout at all,
And there's no one to stamp before,
No one to note his might.
Does he hunch up, as I do,
Against the dark of night?

The Bean Eaters

Inspired especially by Chicago, Brooks wrote many poems about city life, about the prosperous and the poor and the people in between. She noted the injustices everywhere in society, but she also believed in dreams and art. Here, an old man and woman who must survive on very little money nevertheless pass their days with dignity and love for each other. The poet seems to observe them from a distance but sympathizes with them in their situation. A skilled writer, Brooks here combines free verse with rhyme in a relatively novel way.

They eat beans mostly, this old yellow pair.
Dinner is a casual affair.
Plain chipware on a plain and creaking wood,
Tin flatware.

Two who are Mostly Good.
Two who have lived their day,
But keep on putting on their clothes
And putting things away.

And remembering . . .
Remembering, with twinklings and twinges,
As they lean over the beans in their rented back room that
      is full of beads and receipts and dolls and cloths,
        tobacco crumbs, vases and fringes.

yellow—*in this case, very old*
chipware—*plates, saucers, and cups with broken edges*
tin flatware—*cheap knives, forks, and spoons*
fringes—*old-fashioned decorations*

I Want to Write

Margaret Walker (1915–1998)

Born in Birmingham, Alabama, Walker attended Northwestern University near Chicago, where she settled. She came of age as a poet after the Harlem Renaissance but was strongly influenced by its writers, especially Langston Hughes. Her first book of poetry, the prizewinning For My People *(1942), stresses the same note of devotion to African Americans that we see in "I Want to Write." The speaker of the poem is determined to write poetry that will celebrate the lives of "my people," who have "dark hands." Walker does not use rhyme here, but her free verse is by no means loose. Note how she repeats the words "I want" to create an effect like chanting that emphasizes her commitment both to the people and to her art as a poet.*

I want to write
I want to write the songs of my people.
I want to hear them singing melodies in the dark.
I want to catch the last floating strains from their sob-torn
    throats.
I want to frame their dreams into words; their souls into
    notes.
I want to catch their sunshine laughter in a bowl;
fling dark hands to a darker sky
and fill them full of stars
then crush and mix such lights till they become
a mirrored pool of brilliance in the dawn.

☆ ☆ ☆

strains—*tunes*

The Nature of This Flower Is to Bloom

Alice Walker (1944–)

Born in a small town in Georgia, Walker attended school first at Spelman College in Atlanta and then at Sarah Lawrence College near New York City. As a young woman in the age of the civil rights and Black Power movements of the 1960s, she threw herself into a variety of activities that reflected her passionate commitment to the cause of social justice, and perhaps especially to the rights of African American women. Her rising reputation as a writer probably reached its peak in 1982 with the publication of her novel The Color Purple, *which won a Pulitzer Prize. However, Walker was also from the start a dedicated poet who avoided stark confrontational language in favor of a more subtle approach. The speaker in this poem writes in praise of a common but colorful and independent garden flower (a petunia) that, in her mind, knows that it is special and valuable.*

Rebellious. Living.
Against the Elemental Crush.
A Song of Color
Blooming
For Deserving Eyes.
Blooming Gloriously
For its Self.

Revolutionary Petunia.

elemental crush—*rocks and soil, for example*
revolutionary—*in this case, fighting for recognition*

Winter Poem

Nikki Giovanni (1943–)

Of all the younger poets of the Black Power era, which started around 1965, Giovanni was perhaps the most popular and charismatic. Her poetry combined playfulness and humor with militancy—a call to revolution—in a uniquely attractive way that set her apart from other writers. Later she turned steadily from writing political poems to creating works such as "Winter Poem" that nevertheless continued to draw on her lively, attractive, often humorous personality. Here, the speaker of her poem fantasizes about being completely at one with nature. Note how the exuberance of the idea at the core of the poem is shaped by the absence of punctuation and by the frequent, rhythmical use of the words "and" and "I" in a poem that explores the limits of traditional free verse.

once a snowflake fell
on my brow and i loved
it so much and i kissed
it and it was happy and called its cousins
and brothers and a web
of snow engulfed me then
i reached to love them all
and i squeezed them and they became
a spring rain and i stood perfectly
still and was a flower

A Round

· · · · · · · · · · · · · ·

Carolyn M. Rodgers (1940–2010)

Born in Chicago, where she lived most of her life, Rodgers was dedicated to writing poetry that reflected the turbulence of the times and the vitality of life in the African American community. Her use of free verse and also vernacular or popular (street) language combined with her sharp observations about love, politics, human relationships, and other subjects to make her among the most dynamic voices in African American poetry. Here, the speaker of the poem suggests that at times the only way to solve a problem or understand an issue is to wrestle long and hard with it. (A "round" sometimes refers to dancing in a circle or simply to a dance.)

the long way
is often the
short way
for me.
to get where i am going
i sometimes have to end up
in circles

Poem No. 1

Like Dunbar's "We Wear the Mask," this poem in free verse speaks to our frequently perceived need to hide our deepest feelings from the people around us. Perception, however, is not always reality; there are times when we must drop the mask and reach out to others.

our faces are the
light & dark window panes
we paint our smiles on.
behind them,
we hide the vulnerabilities
we want no one else to see.
the water colors of our tears,
even, the rainbows of our laughter . . .
and the heart that can look
through to another heart
might turn away from the face,
    but heart to heart
     as face to face should be
are eyes, that need not hide

vulnerabilities—*weaknesses*

My Father's First Baseball Game

For David
Afaa Michael Weaver (1951–)

Afaa Michael Weaver (born Michael S. Weaver) grew up in Baltimore, Maryland. He studied at the University of Maryland and Brown University in Rhode Island before joining the army. Later he worked at a factory job for many years while he developed as a poet. He is known for the subtlety and tenderness with which he writes about human relationships. In "My Father's First Baseball Game," the speaker's father, who remembers vividly the days before Jackie Robinson when black athletes were not allowed to play baseball in the Major Leagues, attends his first Major League game. To this point he has listened to games on the radio rather than go to a Major League baseball park, where the crowd is likely to be overwhelmingly white. He is caught up in the excitement of the game and forgets the crowd. But his son, the speaker of the poem, cannot bring himself to do so. He knows how much damage racial segregation did to his father's hopes and dreams.

You lumbered along the stadium
like a sinner being marshaled to baptism,
your head high and certain of convictions,
the busy chatter of the crowd beside you.

The radio is better, you declared,
and baseball is baseball regardless.
The wooden seat held you erect and mute,
glancing at the tiny figures in the field.

The open wealth of your first live game
came at you singly as the Negro Leagues
came up, as you spoke of Satchel Paige,
Jackie Robinson, and your ancient radio.

After the ninth, you forgot the crowd,
fingering the ticket stubs in your shirt,
as we floated out into the night
with the deep river of white faces.

marshaled—*led*
the Negro Leagues—*all-black baseball leagues organized because the Major Leagues refused to employ black players*
Satchel Paige—*Paige (1906–1982) was one of the greatest pitchers ever. He played in the Negro Leagues and then (starting in 1948) in the Major Leagues.*
Jackie Robinson—*In 1947, Robinson (1919–1972) became the first black player in the modern era of the Major Leagues.*
the ninth—*usually the last inning in a Major League game*

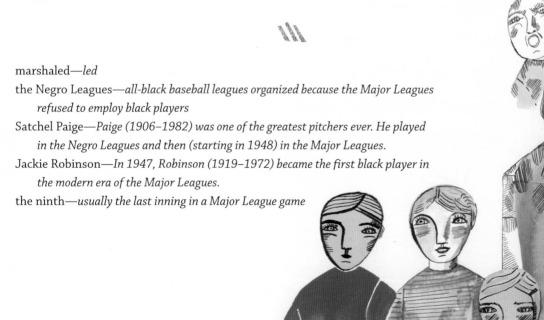

A Meditation for My Son

For Kala

*Weaver seems to suggest that
the speaker in this poem cannot
always control his mind and his
life. In such times when he feels he
is mentally ill, he hopes and prays
that the spirit of his ancestors will
protect his child from danger.*

When I go spinning,
your care is given
to the steel nerves
of reticent angels.

When I cannot hold,
my own heart drops away,
some sure finger from
a faded portrait follows
you in the thorn-filled
curves of man's road.

When I cannot dream,
I pray in blind rooms
that possible colors and bodies
will converge around you,
set you sailing over rocks,
away from the soulless.

When I am not whole,
I entrust you to seraphim
in their difficult dominion.

reticent—*shy*
soulless—*without feeling*
seraph—*a kind of angel*
dominion—*a band of angels*

the poet
....

Lucille Clifton (1936–2010)

*Born in the small town of Depew, New York,
Clifton was brought up by her parents to have
a rich, detailed sense of her family's history,
which they traced back to Dahomey in West
Africa. They also taught her to respect and
even revere the fabric of black social life, about
which she wrote with affection, wit, and in-
sight—and with a special concern for the lives
of women. The author of several volumes of
poetry and also* Generations: A Memoir (*the
story of her family*), *Clifton was one of the
most honored African American writers. Here
the speaker of the poem tells of seeking always
to be calm and controlled in life. However, she
knows that her precious poetry arises typically
from her fears, her joys, and her impulsive spirit.*

i beg my bones to be good but
they keep clicking music and
i spin in the center of myself
a foolish frightful woman
moving my skin against the wind and
tap dancing for my life.

good—*in this case, behaving properly*

Imagination

James Baldwin (1924–1987)

Baldwin, world-famous as a novelist and an essayist, was born in Harlem. Faced with a stepfather who seemed to hate him, he sought relief in public libraries, where he loved to read. A precocious writer, he published his first short story when he was twelve. In 1948, oppressed by conditions in the United States, he moved to Paris, France, but returned frequently in later years, especially during the 1960s and afterward. Baldwin published very few poems. In this work, the speaker of the poem asks puzzling questions. What is real, and what is only myth, the result of one's imagination? Did Columbus really "discover" America, as history books tell us, or did the coming of Europeans (led by Columbus) to America uncover harsh truths about them?

> Imagination
> creates the situation,
> and, then, the situation
> creates imagination.
>
> It may, of course,
> be the other way around:
> Columbus was discovered
> by what he found.

Columbus—*In 1492, the Italian-born explorer Christopher Columbus claimed America on behalf of the king and queen of Spain.*

Caged Bird

Maya Angelou (1928–)

Born Marguerite Ann Johnson in 1928, Angelou grew up in St. Louis, Missouri, the small town of Stamps, Arkansas, and Oakland, California, where she attended high school. This period of her life is central to her most acclaimed work, the bestselling autobiography I Know Why the Caged Bird Sings. *(Its title is taken from a beloved poem by Paul Laurence Dunbar). Talented and adventurous, she excelled in a variety of areas, including dancing, singing, acting, directing, and writing. She published six autobiographies as well as books of poetry and essays that gained her national renown. In 1993, she read one of her poems at the inauguration of President Clinton. For many years she has been an honored professor of American Studies at Wake Forest University in Winston-Salem, North Carolina. "Caged Bird" is one of her most admired poems.*

A free bird leaps
on the back of the wind
and floats downstream
till the current ends
and dips his wing
in the orange sun rays
and dares to claim the sky.

But a bird that stalks
down his narrow cage
can seldom see through
his bars of rage
his wings are clipped and
his feet are tied
so he opens his throat to sing.

The caged bird sings
with a fearful trill
of things unknown
but longed for still
and his tune is heard
on the distant hill
for the caged bird
sings of freedom.

The free bird thinks of another breeze
and the trade winds soft through the sighing trees
and the fat worms waiting on a dawn-bright lawn
and he names the sky his own.

But a caged bird stands on the grave of dreams
his shadow shouts on a nightmare scream
his wings are clipped and his feet are tied
so he opens his throat to sing.

The caged bird sings
with a fearful trill
of things unknown
but longed for still
and his tune is heard
on the distant hill
for the caged bird
sings of freedom.

Alone
. . . .
Michael S. Harper (1938–)

Harper was born in New York City in 1938 but moved with his family to Los Angeles in 1951. He studied at Los Angeles State College, then in the famed Iowa Writers' Workshop at the University of Iowa. Later he became a distinguished professor at Brown University in Providence, Rhode Island. The title of Harper's first book of poetry, Dear John, Dear Coltrane *(1970), suggests his deep attachment to jazz (Coltrane was one of the most brilliant saxophone players in musical history) as well as to African American history and culture in general. To Harper, as to the speaker of his poem, jazz is a complex musical form with precious roots that run deep in African American history. The speaker of his poem dismisses a friend who once liked jazz but now claims to find it inferior as music.*

A friend told me
He'd risen above jazz.
I leave him there.

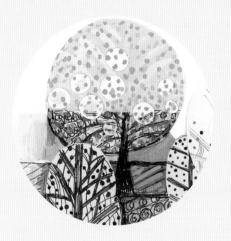

plum blossom plum jam
. . . .
June Jordan (1936–2002)

The child of Jamaican immigrants, Jordan was born in Harlem in New York City. She grew up in a tumultuous household dominated by her father. Her mother eventually committed suicide. Nevertheless, both parents encouraged her to read widely. She was a student at Barnard College in New York City and the University of Chicago. Jordan became a brave fighter for the rights of women and poor people around the world. Eventually she would publish nearly thirty books, including poetry, plays, political essays, and volumes for children and young adults. Of all African American writers of her generation, she was among the most fearless in opposing the forces that harmed people because of their race, nationality, or gender.

plum blossom plum jam
even the tree becomes something
more than a skeleton
longing for the sky

Offspring

Naomi Long Madgett (1923–)

Naomi Long Madgett is a poet and a publisher of poetry. Born in Norfolk, Virginia, she grew up in New Jersey and in St. Louis, Missouri. She attended Virginia State College (now University) and Wayne State University in Detroit. Around 1947 she married and moved to Detroit, where her daughter was born. She taught for many years at Eastern Michigan University. Madgett is also admired for her work with Lotus Press, which publishes poetry by African Americans.

The speaker of her poem "Offspring" discovers that despite her wish to have her daughter live according to the speaker's own hopes and values, the child goes her own way. To the surprise and delight of the speaker, her daughter turns out to be confident, happy, and independent.

I tried to tell her.
  This way the twig is bent.
  Born of my trunk and strengthened by my roots,
  You must stretch newgrown branches
  Closer to the sun
  Than I can reach.
I wanted to say:
  Extend my self to that far atmosphere
  Only my dreams allow.

But the twig broke,
And yesterday I saw her
Walking down an unfamiliar street,
  Feet confident,
  Face slanted upward toward a threatening sky.
  And
  She was smiling
  And she was
  Her very free,
  Her very individual,
  Unpliable
  Own.

offspring—*child*
unpliable—*in this case, independent*

Obsidian

. . . .

For Alvin Aubert
Melvin Dixon (1950–1992)

Dixon was born in Stamford, Connecticut. After graduating from
Wesleyan University, he earned a doctorate in literature at Brown
University. For several years he was a professor at Queens College
in New York. A novelist as well as a poet, he also published a volume
of literary criticism. His poetry reveals not only his learning but
also his highly intelligent and visionary approach to language.
"Obsidian" takes its name from a form of glass that is black in
color and formed by volcanic activity. Extremely hard, it has been
used for arrowheads and as a gemstone.

> Volcanic glass. Smokey shards
> primed and polished. I spew
> from the raging earth
> in all directions. Chilled
> and crystallized, I can become
> religious ornaments in Arizona,
> arrowheads old men call
> Apache tears, or simply
> the cutting
> black edge of a knife.

Apache—*a Native American people*

Apollo

Elizabeth Alexander (1962–)

Alexander is a professor at Yale University in New Haven, Connecticut. She is also a graduate of Yale, Boston University, and the University of Pennsylvania, where she earned a doctorate in literature. An acclaimed writer, she was chosen by President Obama to read one of her poems at his inauguration in 2009. Her poem "Apollo" takes us back to July 20, 1969, when men landed on the moon for the first time. The U.S. spacecraft Eagle *touched down with Apollo 11 astronauts Neil Armstrong and Edwin "Buzz" Aldrin, Jr. Eager to watch the event on television, an African American family traveling by car stops at a roadside restaurant frequented by white customers. For a moment, the drama on the screen seems to put racial tension in its proper perspective.*

We pull off
to a road shack
in Massachusetts
to watch men walk

on the moon. We did
the same thing
for three two one
blast off, and now

we watch the same men
bounce in and out
of craters. I want
a Coke and a hamburger.

Because the men
are walking on the moon
which is now irrefutably
not green, not cheese,

not a shiny dime floating
in a cold blue,
the way I'd thought,
the road shack people don't

notice we are a black
family not from there,
the way it mostly goes.
This talking through

static, bounces in space-
boots, tethered
to cords is much
stranger, stranger

even than we are.

My People

Langston Hughes

The night is beautiful,
So the faces of my people.

The stars are beautiful,
So the eyes of my people.

Beautiful, also, is the sun.
Beautiful, also, are the souls of my people.

Index